Tog the Sporty Dog

Colin and Jacqui Hawkins

FAMILY LEARNING

Exercise is fun for everyone!

FAMILY LEARNING

from Dorling Kindersley

The Family Learning mission is to support the concept of the home as a centre of learning and to help families develop independent learning skills to last a lifetime.

Editors: Bridget Gibbs, Fiona Munro
Designers: Chris Fraser, Lisa Hollis

Published by Family Learning

Dorling Kindersley registered offices:
9 Henrietta Street, Covent Garden, London WC2E 8PS

www.dk.com

4 6 8 10 9 7 5 3

ISBN 0-7513-7109-2

Colour reproduction by DOT Gradations
Printed in Hong Kong by Wing King Tong

A CIP catalogue record for this book is
available from the British Library.

Do you know about Tog?
"I'm a very sporty dog," said Tog.
One day he went out for a jog.

Tog met his friend, Hog.
"Hi, Hog. Come for a jog," said Tog.
"No thanks, Tog. Hogs don't jog like dogs,"
said Hog. "It's too much of a slog."
"That's not true, jogging's good for you.
Come and run, it's great fun," said Tog.

"Well, I am a little bit fat," said Hog.
"I'll soon get rid of that," said Tog the dog.
"Come on, let's jog, you lazy Hog."

"If I'm going to get you fit,
you'll need some new sports kit,"
said Tog the dog to Hog.
At the sports shop
there was lots to choose.
Hog bought himself
some running shoes.

Then Tog took Hog to the sports hall to play a game of basketball.
"I'm too short for this sport," said Hog as Tog whizzed around the court.

"Exercise is great, it keeps
down your weight," said Tog.
"Doing gym is very tough.
I've already had quite enough!"
said Hog to Tog the sporty dog.

"You don't like the gym, so how about a swim? That will make you trim," said Tog.
"But the water's chilly," said Hog.
"Don't be silly," said Tog.

Then he gave a big grin and pushed Hog in.
SPLOSH!

Hog was now tired and hot, but Tog the sporty dog was **not**.
"1, 2, 3, skip like me!" said Tog with glee.
"I'm puffed out," said Hog.
"You're still too stout!"
said Tog.

"Let's go and skate!" said sporty Tog.
"But it's getting late!" said poor tired Hog.
"I'll race you," said Tog and off he flew.
Poor Hog was in a state, he couldn't skate
and Tog the dog wouldn't wait!

"I think you'll like tennis," said Tog.
Hog said, "Tog, you're a menace!"
With a WHACK! and a SMACK!
Tog served an ace and hit Hog in the face!

Hog was so upset,
he tied Tog up in the net.
"What a catch! Game, set and
match!" said Hog to Tog the
sporty dog.

"I don't want to be fit or thinner.
I just want my dinner. NOW!" said Hog.
"OK, you win," said Tog, with a grin.
"You've done your best, you need a rest."

"I'm ready to drop, please can we stop!" puffed Hog. "Here's just the place to put a smile on your face," said Tog the sporty dog, as they came to a café that was open all day.

"It all looks a treat, what
will you eat?" asked Tog.
"I'll have soup in a bowl
with a big buttered roll,
a pizza with cheese
and tomato, please.
I'd like to try to eat
a whole apple pie,
then a chocolate cake
and a big milkshake,"
said hungry Hog to
Tog the sporty dog.

As Tog watched Hog chew and chew, he said "I know just the sport for you! Food's the thing that you like best – this will put you to the test!"

Said Hog to Tog, "What sport can that be?"
But Tog just smiled and said, "Follow me!"

"Here's a clue," Tog said at last.
"There's lots of food,
but you must run fast."

"Hog, grab a pan and run as fast as you can," said Tog. Suddenly it all became clear. "It's a pancake race!" said Hog with a cheer! **"Get ready! Get steady! Go Hog, Go!"** shouted Tog, **"Don't be slow!"**

Hog ran so fast he thought he would fly, tossing his pancake high in the sky. He was first over the line, in double quick time!